THE KARATE PRINCESS
TO THE RESCUE

Princess Belinda has had enough of boring old piano lessons at home. She's chopped up the piano, and is looking for adventure. When she hears that her karate teacher has been imprisoned by the evil warlord, Utagawa, she sets off to Japan to rescue him.

But for once it looks like the daredevil princess herself is in trouble. Her karate skills have no effect on Utagawa's army of sumo wrestlers and Belinda is powerless. Is this the end for the Karate Princess, or is anyone brave enough to attempt her rescue?

This is the third adventure story featuring the Karate Princess.

Jeremy Strong has been writing for children for fifteen years. He lives in Kent with his wife, two teenagers (who have tried out all his stories), one cat, one dog, five guinea pigs, three goldfish and a spider in the kitchen called Wittgenstein.

The Karate Princess to the Rescue

Jeremy Strong

Illustrated by Simone Abel

PUFFIN BOOKS

PUFFIN BOOKS

Published by the Penguin Group
Penguin Books Ltd, 27 Wrights Lane, London w8 5tz, England
Penguin Books USA Inc., 375 Hudson Street, New York, New York 10014, USA
Penguin Books Australia Ltd, Ringwood, Victoria, Australia
Penguin Books Canada Ltd, 10 Alcorn Avenue, Toronto, Ontario, Canada m4v 3b2
Penguin Books (NZ) Ltd, 182–190 Wairau Road, Auckland 10, New Zealand

Penguin Books Ltd, Registered Offices: Harmondsworth, Middlesex, England

First published by A & C Black 1991
Published in Puffin Books 1993
1 3 5 7 9 10 8 6 4 2

Text copyright © Jeremy Strong, 1991
Illustrations copyright © Simone Abel, 1991
All rights reserved

The moral right of the author has been asserted

Typeset by Datix International Limited, Bungay, Suffolk
Filmset in Lasercomp Bembo
Printed in England by Clays Ltd, St Ives plc

I

Bad News from Tobi-shima

Plink plonk crunch. Plunk plank crash bang! This strange mishmash of noise was quickly followed by a scream of rage. 'Aaargh!' Princess Belinda erupted from the piano stool and stamped up and down the room. 'I hate the piano,' she seethed. 'It's a stupid instrument.'

The Queen eyed her daughter fondly. 'Never mind dear. I'm sure there are lots of easier instruments to learn.' This remark only annoyed Belinda more. She swung round, eyes glaring.

'I see, so you think the piano is too difficult for me do you? It's not me that's stupid, it's the piano!'

'Of course it is dear,' the Queen went on mildly. 'I was simply pointing out that there are easier instruments – the triangle for example. Why don't you learn the triangle?'

Princess Belinda drew herself up to her full height, which was not very tall, and fixed her mother with a withering look. She took a deep breath. 'One more go,' she muttered. 'One more go just to show you that I can do it.' Belinda fetched the piano stool from where she had last kicked it, halfway up the Grand Staircase, and sat down. Screwing up her face into an intense mask of concentration she began to push the piano keys with her fingers. Plink plink plunk scrunch! Plonk plink plonk spludge!

'Aaaaaargh!' This time the stool went all the way to the top of the Grand Staircase as Belinda leapt to her feet. Her hands slowly circled the air, palms and fingers held out flat and straight. Belinda drew breath sharply and closed in on the huge three-legged piano-monster.

The Queen was also on her feet. 'Oh dear,' she murmured. She had seen her daughter like this before, and knew just what it meant. 'Belinda darling,' she began hastily, 'I know the piano has been rather difficult but don't you . . .'

But it was no use – her voice was drowned out by a deafening bang as Belinda spun on one foot and launched a devastating series of high karate kicks at the unfortunate instrument. It plunged to its belly as the legs splintered. Belinda jumped back, drawing power back into her hands. 'Ha-aaaa-aaaAAA-AKK!!' Her right hand flashed in a mighty curve and chopped the huge belly in half. A hundred piano wires snapped and pinged off in different directions. A hundred keys flew like an exploding chip basket and clattered across the palace floor.

Belinda bowed deeply to the dead beast and calmly sat down in an armchair, hardly even panting. A smile came to her face. Her mother stood by the wrecked piano and shook her head.

'Oh dear. You know Belinda, I thought karate was supposed to teach you patience and control. I'm afraid your father isn't going to be pleased when he sees what you've done. That's two violins, a trombone, a double bass and a piano you've destroyed in less than a week.'

'I don't care. I've given up,' said Belinda. 'It was a stupid idea of Hubert's anyway. I don't know why I went along with it. First of all he tried to get me to paint. Just because he's an artist he thinks everyone else can be too!'

'You did manage to prove him wrong quite quickly,' the Queen pointed out.

'Well he never said you only had to squeeze those tubes of paint gently. It wasn't my fault the crimson went straight in his eye.'

'No of course it wasn't dear, and after all, he did forgive you, didn't he? But I think it was later on, when you somehow managed to squeeze charcoal black in his ear, yellow all down his front and shampoo his hair with the leaf green that he began to lose his patience.'

Belinda snorted. 'It was his own stupid fault. Why am I doing this for him anyway? Why am I trying to please him?' An enormously soppy smile spread across the Queen's face. Belinda took one look and rolled her eyes. 'No mother, I am not in love with Hubert and I never shall be in love with Hubert and I am not going to marry him, or anyone else, ever. Men are so . . . stupid!'

'I never said a word dear,' murmured the Queen with grave innocence.

'Good. I'm going to the garden to find Knackerleevee. At least he understands me.' Belinda jumped to her feet and stalked out to the garden. Knackerleevee was sitting in the grass by the trees trying to make a daisy chain. This was a very difficult task for a Bogle from The Marsh at the End of the World. His gigantic fingernails and hairy hands made the job almost impossible. He grunted and scratched his shaggy belly.

Belinda went up behind the great creature and leaned over his massive shoulders. 'I know just how you feel,' she said.

'I can't get the hang of it, Highness Person. It looks so easy,' growled the Bogle.

Belinda nodded. 'That's what I thought, watching Hubert paint. And then, when I saw him playing the piano I thought that was easy too.'

'Hubert's clever,' said Knackerleevee. Belinda was silent. 'Very clever,' Knackerleevee added. 'He's got brains.'

Belinda smiled and nodded. She picked up a

broken tree branch from the grass. It was thick and heavy. She held it out to the Bogle. 'Hold this,' she said. 'Go on, hold it out.' Knackerleevee grinned and held out the branch at arm's length. Belinda drew back one hand.

'Ha-akk!' A single quick blow split the branch neatly in two. Belinda watched the two sections fall to the grass.

'Hubert's clever, but he can't do that,' she said, and they both began to laugh. Suddenly Belinda's laughter turned to a surprised shriek.

'Did you see that?' she cried grabbing the Bogle's arm and staring up at the sky.

'What?'

'That. I think it was a bird,' Belinda said, still staring at the sky. Knackerleevee shook his head.

'There are lots of birds. Which one do you mean Princessness? There's a brown one there, and a black one with a yellow . . .'

Belinda clutched his arm once more. 'There – look! Too late, it's gone. I've never seen a bird fly so fast. First of all it went across that way and then it went the other and look – there it is again.'

They both saw it the third time, though hardly long enough to say what it was other than a bird flying incredibly fast. Then suddenly it whizzed across the palace roofs, skidded violently to one side and came down straight at them in a scream-ing dive. Belinda and the Bogle ducked as the bird came crashing through the trees, scattering leaves on all sides. Finally it burst from the foliage and thudded straight into the Bogle's chest. He tottered for a second, then keeled over backwards, all the breath knocked from his huge body.

Belinda stared at the fallen ogre. Lying beside him, with eyes going round and round like mad aniseed balls was a large black crow. Knacker-leevee groaned and sat up. 'What was THAT?' he asked.

Belinda bent down and lifted the bird on to her arm. 'It's a crow,' she said. 'Although I've never seen a crow quite like it anywhere.'

The crow groaned and moved its wings feebly. The big beak opened once or twice, and a hoarse voice came from the scrawny body. 'Where am I? Is this Heaven? Am I dead?' The crow suddenly sat bolt upright, eyes wide, staring at herself. 'I AM dead! I'm dead! I've got wings! I'm an angel! I'm in Heaven!'

Princess Belinda coughed gently. 'I'm sorry to disappoint you but you're not in Heaven and you're not dead. You have just crashed into one of my best friends and you are in the palace garden of my father, King Stormbelly.'

The crow dug her sharp talons into Belinda's arm. 'King Stormbelly? Then I have reached my journey's end. I have crossed mountains and deserts. I have crossed the seven seas and braved the roar of the hurricane. I have dodged the great eagles and flown blind through sandstorms. I . . .'

Belinda tapped the crow on one shoulder.

'Look, just get on with it will you. Why were you trying to find us?' The crow drew herself up proudly and half closed her glittering eyes.

'I am one of the famous Kamikaze Crows of Japan. I have been trained. I speak! I fly! I count – but only up to thirteen. I have flown thousands of miles to bring you a message from Japan, from my ancient master Hiro Ono.'

Belinda almost fainted with surprise. 'Hiro Ono? My master Hiro Ono who taught me all I know about karate?'

'Just so,' said Crow. 'He's my master too. He taught me to speak and . . .' Crow slithered further up Belinda's arm, nearer the trees. 'He also taught me – haaaa-akk!'

A small twig snapped from the lightning blow it got from Crow's wing. 'You see, I am a deadly karate expert.' He muttered this as if it was the most dangerous secret in the world. Belinda bit her lip to try and stop herself from laughing.

'But what is the message from my master?' asked Belinda. 'Why have you flown all this way from Japan?' Crow hid her head beneath one wing.

'I'm too ashamed to tell you. It wasn't my fault . . . I couldn't help it.'

'Couldn't help what?'

'There were too many of them. They came in the night.'

'Who? What?' asked Belinda desperately.

'The evil sumo wrestlers of Tobi-shima. They came in the night and took away Hiro Ono. He is a prisoner in the warlord's castle. They will kill him if he doesn't teach them his karate secrets. But if he does, the whole of Japan will be unsafe. The evil sumo wrestlers will know how to do sumo *and* karate – they'll be like rhinoceroses with the bite of cobra snakes. Hiro Ono has sent me to find the Little Daughter of Earthquake.'

Belinda smiled. 'That's what he called me.'

'I know,' said Crow. 'I have seen the piano. Hiro Ono needs you to come to Japan and rescue him. It's not just for his sake, but for the whole of Japan.'

'This sounds like the kind of adventure I've been waiting for. Come on Knackerleevee, let's find Hubert and get going.'

Crow glanced at the Bogle and coughed rudely. 'You're not bringing that rug on legs are you?' The Bogle growled and Crow ducked her head under one wing.

'Yes,' laughed Belinda. 'I never go anywhere without my fur rug, and Hubert of course. Come on, let's go and rescue my old master, Hiro Ono. This could be . . . interesting!'

All at Sea

Belinda's father, King Stormbelly, could hardly believe what he was hearing. 'Do you mean to tell me you're waltzing off to Japan with a talking bird?'

'Yes father. It's about time I did something useful.'

'Exactly,' snapped the King. 'You are a royal princess Belinda, and almost twenty years old. Royal princesses do not go around smashing up pianos and travelling abroad with talking birds. You are supposed to . . .'

'Stay at home, get married and die of boredom,' Belinda interrupted.

'Exactly. Yes, I mean no! Of course you don't die of boredom. Your mother was a princess. She married me. She hasn't died of boredom has she?'

The Queen yawned gracefully and smiled at her husband. 'Sorry dear,' she murmured, and winked at Belinda. The princess took her father's hand and patted it gently.

'We shan't be gone long Daddy. We must go and rescue Hiro Ono. I owe so much to him.'

Crow swooped down on to King Stormbelly's shoulder and cawed loudly in his ear. 'Hiro Ono is a great karate expert. He taught me, Haa-So!' The bird snapped one wing and the royal crown went spinning like some ancient flying saucer across the room. 'Oops! Very sorry,' said Crow. 'I don't know my own strength.'

The king grunted, picked up his crown and returned it carefully to his head. He turned back to his daughter, clearly trying to stay calm. 'I have had second thoughts,' he said, fixing Crow with a murderous glare. 'And my second thoughts are that the sooner you take this lunatic bird away from here the better, and the further you take her away the better. If by some chance she meets with a terrible accident I shan't mind in the least – but do take care of yourself Belinda.'

Belinda rushed forward and gave her father an enormous hug. 'I knew you'd agree in the end. We'll find Hubert, pack what we need and be off straight away.'

Hubert was standing still and silent at the top of the castle's tallest tower. He was gazing at the vast expanse of sky, watching the steadily changing clouds and wondering how he could capture their beauty on canvas. In one hand was an almost dry paintbrush. His rapture was only broken when Belinda came hurtling up the stairs like a human whirlwind, closely followed by the lumbering figure of Knackerleevee. A black rocket screamed past Hubert's left ear and appeared to explode in the sky just above him.

'You can't take him!' screamed Crow. 'We need a fierce and brave warrior not some weedy young artist who paints pictures of clouds!'

'Sssh,' said Belinda, 'you'll hurt his feelings.'

Crow ignored the princess and flew down to Hubert, perching on his easel.

'Can you do karate?' Crow demanded.

'No, but . . .'

'Haaaa-so!' One wing flashed and a paintbrush snapped in half and fell to the stone floor.

'Hey,' began Hubert. 'That's . . .'

'Can you fight?' squawked Crow.

'No, but . . .'

'Haaaa-SO!' Another brush fell in two. Hubert picked up the pieces carefully.

'Now look here,' he began.

'Can you splurrgh urkkk!' Crow suddenly found two tubes of paint rammed into her beak. She squirmed and wriggled and finally spat them out. 'That wasn't very nice,' she muttered.

'Well I don't like anyone, or anyTHING for

that matter, breaking my paintbrushes and telling me I'm weedy,' said Hubert. 'What's more I'll have you know that if there's an adventure ahead then I'm coming too and if you don't like it you can . . .'

The Karate Princess watched Hubert with a smile. 'You know Hubert, I've never seen you lose your temper before. You're always so calm. It's one of the things I like about you.'

Hubert blushed. He covered his embarrassment by noisily packing up his painting gear. 'Where are we going?' he asked, and then became very excited when Belinda told him. 'Japan! The Orient! I've always wanted to go there – and a sea journey too!'

After travelling for three days they reached the coast and finally managed to hire a boat. It was quite small, but strongly built and could be easily managed by the three of them. It had one small cannon, just in case they ran into trouble.

They were all desperately impatient to get going, but even so it took them nearly a whole day to find their way out of the harbour. It was only a small harbour, but none of them had sailed before. Crow was up in the crow's nest of course, yelling out directions. 'Left a bit, bit more, NO! Right, right quickly, now back a bit, slow down, back a bit, back, Back, BACK!!!'

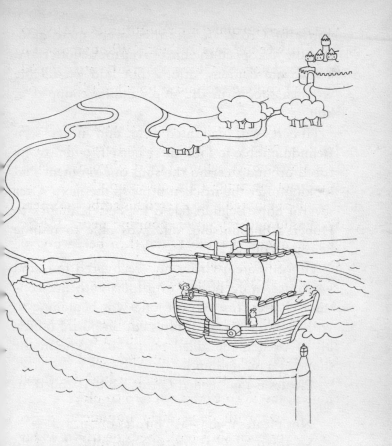

There was a crunch and Crow fell from the nest for the twenty-third time. But at last everyone seemed to get the hang of it and as the sun set over the glistening sea the little boat sailed out of the harbour and ventured on to the mighty ocean.

Belinda immediately went down with raging sea-sickness. So did Crow. Nobody took much notice of Crow. In fact they were quite glad, because it stopped the bird's constant chatter and her karate demonstrations that had left all the wooden spoons in the ship's galley chopped in half.

Hubert was delighted. He had never seen Belinda unable to look after herself, and now he raced around steering the ship one moment and looking after the stricken princess the next. After several days Belinda felt a lot better, thanks to Hubert's fine nursing, and was able to resume her duties on deck.

Unfortunately Crow had recovered too, and was once more boring everyone with her constant chatter. Just as everyone was beginning to wish that there was a ship's cat on board a little bit of excitement sailed on to the scene in the shape of a pirate ship.

'Pirates a-joy!' yelled Crow. Hubert rolled his eyes.

'Not pirates a-joy – it's pirates ahoy.'

'So sorry,' said Crow sarcastically, 'but I do not think it matters. We are all going to be killed anyway. The pirates are armed to the teeth. We're going to die. Goodbye, Toodle-pip. HELP!!!'

While Crow jumped up and down in her nest Belinda rubbed her hands together. She watched the pirate vessel closing fast. 'I'm going to enjoy this,' she murmured. Hubert smiled.

'I feel sorry for them already. If you don't mind I'll join Crow up there and do some lightning sketches. Knowing you, this won't take long to sort out.'

A moment later the two ships came together. Thirty dirty bearded faces came swinging across on ropes. Crow was right. They were armed to the teeth. Not only that but some were armed to the knees. They all had nasty sharp swords and knives, except the youngest and newest member who had a potato peeler. Captain Deadhead, a fierce-looking bearded man with a green eye patch, (he was colour blind), saw Crow and grinned. 'Arrr, a parrot to be sure, and a right scurvy parrot for a brave pirate captain such as meself!' he roared. (He was not only colour blind but immensely stupid as well.) He made a grab for the bird.

Crow gave a yelp of terror, left three tail feathers behind and hastily flew off and hid down the cannon. Meanwhile, Belinda and Knacker-leevee stood quietly on the quarterdeck and waited. The pirates came surging forward. 'Good morning gentlemen,' said Belinda calmly.

Captain Deadhead bristled and glared at the slip of a girl that stood in his path. 'Well me hearties, look what we have here. A lily-livered landlubber to be sure, and I'll have her guts for garters in a second or two!' He swished his

massive sword through the air, forcing his fellow
pirates to leap back several feet to avoid having
their heads chopped off.

'Good morning,' repeated Belinda with quiet
menace. 'I'm sorry to say this, but if you don't
return to your ship at once you won't find your
ship, or yourselves in one piece.'

Captain Deadhead roared with laughter. Suddenly he stopped and thrust his face in front of
Belinda. 'Get out of my way little girl, before I
slice you up like a bit of cheap salami. I know
you. You're the Karate Princess. My brother told
me about you.'

'Your brother?'

'Yes. He used to be leader of the Cut-throat Robbers. He's given it all up to become an ice-cream salesman. What a little girly. He's not tough like me, you know – I'll make mincemeat of you.'

Belinda eyed the pirate captain steadily. She drew in her breath slowly. She drew back one arm. 'Aaaaa-ukk!' Deadhead slid slowly to the deck, a ridiculous smile on his unconscious face. 'Typical man,' murmured Belinda. 'Nothing but talk.'

Twenty-nine pirates muttered angrily and pressed forward. The door behind the princess opened and Knackerleevee stepped out. 'Shall we begin Princessy?' he asked with a grin, and they waded into the remaining pirates.

Some went flying one way and some the other. Some had two black eyes, and the lucky ones had one. There was an awful lot of noise, most of it cries or screams of surprise, and eventually there were no conscious pirates left on board.

Knackerleevee and Belinda bowed solemnly to each other. They picked up the bodies and flung them back on to the pirate ship. To make sure the pirates couldn't harm anyone else Belinda loaded the cannon.

There was a big bang. Out shot Crow, feathers

flying in every direction, closely followed by a cannon ball that ripped through the pirate ship. It began to sink rapidly.

Crow settled on Knackerleevee's head and smoothed her feathers. Even being blown from her hiding place didn't stop her yacking. She began to dance round and round. 'Did you see me? Did you see what I did? I went AKK! and UKK! Did you see me send that fat pirate spinning into the sea? Did you see me break that giant pirate's leg?'

Belinda, Knackerleevee and Hubert looked at each other and then at Crow. 'No,' they said in unison. 'We didn't.'

'Oh.' Crow quietened down considerably. 'Well I must have been too fast for you. Think I'll go and see if there are any spoons left in the kitchen.'

3

All is Revealed

The gallant ship sailed on, and on and on. Knack-erleevee thought he would die from listening to the non-stop yacking of Crow. Belinda thought she would die of boredom. Hubert stood on deck and painted different views of the heaving sea. By the time they neared Japan he had finished sixty-four paintings.

Sometimes Crow went off scouting for land. She would come back with tales of her daring adventures, such as the time she was swallowed by a whale. 'I managed to wedge open the beast's jaw with my incredibly strong wings and squeeze out.'

'Yes,' muttered Knackerleevee, 'and my mother is the fairy on top of the Christmas tree.'

Crow's beak fell open. 'Really?' she said, the Bogle's joke quite lost on her, but it brought a smile to Belinda's face. At that moment Hubert gave a joyful cry.

'Land! Land ahoy! It's Japan at last. We've arrived!'

It was true, and as if to help them along a fresh

breeze suddenly caught the sails and the little boat sailed into the harbour. As they tied up at the jetty they noticed a young man in tunic and armour standing at the end of the wooden pier. He was watching them closely. They had hardly left the ship and walked five steps when he blocked their way, planting his legs wide apart. In a single flash he drew his sword and there followed an extraordinary display. It was like a ballet, but with a deadly sword whistling through the air which cut and sliced in beautiful graceful patterns. Then all at once there was a quiet 'shoooosh', and the sword was back in its case.

The young warrior stepped forward and bowed low. 'Welcome to my country and the country of my father. I am Hiro Junior, son of Hiro Ono, and Samurai warrior to our master,

Lord Oko of Nozoki.' The handsome young man straightened and smiled at everyone.

He took Belinda's hand and raised it to his lips. 'You must be the Karate Princess. My father has told me many things about you, Little Daughter of Earthquake.'

Belinda blushed slightly. 'Tell us about your father,' she said. 'Is he all right?' Hiro Junior smiled again.

'My father always said you worry about other people, and never about yourself. My father is all right, but he is a prisoner of Lord Utagawa.'

Crow suddenly arrived on Hiro Junior's shoulder. 'Lord Utagawa!' she hissed. 'I'll kill him with one blow, Haaa . . .' But before Crow could raise one wing Hiro Junior reached up and grabbed her by the neck.

'I see my father's bird found you and that she still hasn't stopped boasting.' Hiro Junior rattled off something to Crow in very fast Japanese and let the bird go. Crow gave a squawk of terror and snapped her beak shut with a loud clack. Hiro Junior turned back to his new friends. 'I've told Crow that if she opens her beak once more I'll give her to my mother.'

Seeing how Crow was still trembling from this terrible threat nobody dared ask Hiro Junior what was so dreadful about his mother. Hiro Junior went on. 'My father calls Crow "Little

Bird with Running Tongue". He also calls her many other things but they're far too rude to say in polite company.' Belinda gave a little giggle and Hubert, walking just behind, felt an unexpected hotness all over that made him angry and annoyed.

'Tell us more about your father,' said Belinda.

'Not far from here is an island called Tobi-shima. It belongs to the warlord Utagawa. He is a very bad man. He wants to rule all Japan. He wants slaves and great riches. Many years ago there was a big battle. My master, Lord Oko of Nozoki, won the battle and banished Utagawa to the island of Tobi-shima where he couldn't be of any harm. But that was a long time ago. Utagawa is a clever man, and over the years he has gathered an army of evil sumo wrestlers. The army is the biggest in Japan, and the most dangerous.'

'What are sumo wrestlers?' Belinda asked.

Hiro Junior smiled. 'You will see. Look, we have arrived at the palace of Nozoki.' Huge

wooden gates opened before them and the party walked up a long clean path to the palace. It was quite unlike anything Belinda had expected. It was like a gigantic bungalow with small towers at each corner. Everywhere they went people bowed low to them. Knackerleevee thought it was quite wonderful and kept stopping to bow back. 'They must think I'm a Highship person like you,' he said to Belinda.

They mounted the palace steps and just as Belinda began to wonder how they could get in because there didn't appear to be any doors, Hiro Junior slid back one of the walls. 'That's brilliant,' she cried. 'A door that goes sideways.'

'Please, take off your shoes. We have slippers for you. It is a custom in Japan. Now we will see Lord Oko.'

They went through to a grand hall. Rows of Samurai warriors lined one side, and on the other were all the women, in beautiful silk kimonos. The friends walked slowly up the aisle between

everyone. At the far end was a massive chair and seated on it the imposing figure of Lord Oko.

Belinda and Hubert could not help glancing at each other and raising their eyebrows, for Lord Oko looked exactly like a Japanese version of King Stormbelly. He was short and fat and had bad-temper wrinkles across his forehead and around the corners of his mouth. They bowed low before him and Hiro Junior spoke.

'My master, I bring you a great karate warrior from far away, a pupil of my father Hiro Ono. Belinda, the Karate Princess, or, as my father calls her, Little Daughter of Earthquake.'

Lord Oko watched Belinda with a severe frown. 'Come,' he growled and she walked up the steps to his throne. He stretched out a thick hand and grabbed one wrist. Then he squeezed. He squeezed her arm muscles and pinched her cheeks. He made her open her mouth and he examined her teeth. Belinda was rapidly losing her temper.

'Do you mind! I'm not a sack of potatoes you know!'

'Quiet!' snapped Lord Oko. A gasp of horror went up from everyone at the court. Nobody spoke to Lord Oko like that. He pushed Belinda away from him. 'You are too small,' he announced.

Belinda put her hands on her hips. Hubert closed his eyes and began to pray. He knew something awful was about to happen. Knacker-leevee grinned madly and whispered under his breath, 'Go on Princessyness, you show the old dustbag.'

The Karate Princess looked round the room. Just behind Lord Oko was a nice clean wall. She took a deep breath and concentrated her inner strength. Then she spun on one foot and hurled herself forward.

'Belinda . . .' yelled Hiro Junior, but it was too late. With a thundering yell Belinda crashed through the wall. Instead of the sound of bricks flying everywhere as she had expected, all there came was the sound of tearing paper. With so much power behind her Belinda went whizzing through the paper wall, straight across the floor of the room beyond, right through another paper wall and slap bang into the middle of a chicken run.

Chickens flew away, clucking madly. A

featherstorm burst around her head. As she sat there Belinda could feel dozens of eggs slowly empty their contents all over her.

A few moments later, Hiro Junior poked his face through the torn paper wall. He shook his head as he reached in and pulled the messy princess from the chicken run. 'I tried to warn you. The walls in Japan are not made of bricks. We make our walls from paper.'

'Paper walls,' murmured Belinda, squelching across the floor. 'I should have known. Sliding doors and paper walls.'

The great hall was filled with a terrible silence as everyone waited to see what Lord Oko would do about the terrible girl who had wrecked his palace walls. His face was a pure thunderstorm. The Karate Princess squelched back into the hall, with bits of shell slowly sliding down her and scrambled eggs everywhere.

Lord Oko raised his eyes and fixed them upon Belinda. For a moment he said nothing. Then he seemed to choke. He coughed, he spluttered, he heaved, and then everyone realized he was starting to laugh. A moment later huge bellows broke from him and at this signal the entire court started to laugh with him.

Belinda looked at them all. She looked at herself, and she began to laugh too. She saw all the warriors laughing and went down to join them. She laughed with the first one. 'Ha ha ha haaa akk!' He slumped to the ground. She laughed with the second one. A moment later he slumped down unconscious. He was quickly joined by five more. By this time the other warriors had got the message and the laughter died on their faces. They tried to look very serious.

Belinda picked up all the dented helmets, carried them to Lord Oko and threw them at his feet. He stopped laughing too. 'I have come thousands of miles to help my master Hiro Ono,' said Belinda quietly. 'You may have many warriors in your army Lord Oko, but Hiro Ono would not have sent for me if your warriors could have freed him. Now I suggest that you tell me about the sumo wrestlers of Tobi-shima and where my master is being held prisoner and then I can get on with rescuing him.'

Lord Oko watched Belinda's blue eyes steadily. 'Many people think it's brave and clever to smash bricks with their hand – or walls,' he added with a sly smile. 'But it is far braver to speak to Lord Oko like this. You have great courage, Little Daughter of Earthquake. Hiro Ono was right to send for you. Sit here by me.' Lord Oko clapped his hands. 'Fetch Little Daughter some clean clothes. Drag those guards away and wake them up. Make our brave guests welcome.'

There was a rush of action as the orders were put into effect. 'Now I'll show you what sumo wrestlers are,' said Lord Oko. 'The warlord Uta-gawa has many sumos, and they are very danger-ous.' He reached to one side, picked up a small gong, and gave it a single blow with the hammer.

Two large screens were pushed back. Lord Oko clapped his hands and two hugely fat men stomped on to the big wrestling mat. Belinda gasped and covered her face.

'Oh,' she said. 'They're . . ., they're . . .'

'Fat?' suggested Lord Oko.

'No!' squeaked Belinda, turning extremely red. 'They're all bare!'

4

Grand Plans

'Not quite,' said Hiro Junior, joining them. 'See, they're wearing special sumo trunks with tassels. Watch.'

Belinda opened her fingers a little and peeped through the gap. Now she could see that both wrestlers were wearing what looked like gigantic bandages, wrapped round their loins. Even so she could still see their great fat bottoms and wasn't quite sure where to look.

The two old men grunted and bowed to each other. They crouched down, knees bent, their

huge fat stomachs spilling outwards, and their hands held up like gigantic lobster claws. Hubert, Belinda and Knackerleevee watched spellbound. The Bogle whispered in Belinda's ear. 'This reminds me of The Marsh at the End of the World. Bogles fight like this. But these men are too old.'

It was true. They had long wispy beards and their fat bodies were not just wrinkled from too much flesh, but were crinkled with old age. You could almost hear their bones creaking as they slowly moved towards each other.

Suddenly there was a violent slap of flesh as the two aged mountains hurled themselves together. The ground shook beneath the audience. Grunts and hisses filled the air as the two men struggled to get a good grip on each other. The locked pair slowly twisted and stamped and snorted.

Belinda still had both hands in front of her face. 'You can see half their bottoms,' she murmured.

'Somehow I am reminded of your mother's dumpling stew,' Hubert replied. 'What are they actually trying to do?'

Lord Oko frowned. 'Watch,' he repeated, pointing at the wrestlers. The two wrestlers started trying to lift each other from the floor. Slowly they began to move across the mat, panting and heaving. At last one, with a superhuman effort, lifted his opponent from the floor. Unfortunately the sheer weight was too much and the old man toppled backwards, with the other on top. There was an almighty thud as they hit the floor, and both lay there unable to do anything more except groan.

Lord Oko sat back with satisfaction and clapped his hands. Four stretcher bearers trotted on to the wrestling mat. They shovelled the two wrestlers on to the stretchers and carried them away to receive immediate first aid. Hiro Junior smiled.

'Now you see our problem. These men are too old to wrestle and too old to teach us. The sumo wrestlers of Tobi-shima are much bigger and as strong as elephants. They have arms that can crush the life from a body like a python snake round a mouse.'

Princess Belinda paused thoughtfully. 'What

about karate? Hasn't your father taught the palace soldiers karate?'

'Of course,' snapped Hiro Junior. 'We are the finest karate warriors in Japan.'

Something large and black suddenly appeared from nowhere. There was a flash of wing. 'Haaaaa–akk!' The gong clanged on to the floor. Crow flew down and pounced on it. She drew in her feathers. 'I am the danger that stalks the invisible air,' she began. 'I strike when you least expect it. No one is safe from urrrk!' Crow gave a strangled squawk as Lord Oko seized her by the neck and flung her into a cage. He passed a cloth over the cage. There were a few squawks of rage, then silence.

'Crow talks too much,' said Lord Oko. 'But she is stupid. Now she thinks it is night because it is dark. She will sleep.'

'If only we'd known that trick before,' mused Hubert. 'We could have saved ourselves all that boredom.'

Hiro Junior nodded and went on. 'The sumo wrestlers of Tobi-shima are big and strong. They are even fatter than the old men you've just seen. Karate is very difficult to use with them. It's like hitting a piece of cotton wool.'

Belinda sat down. 'I see the problem. It makes the island very difficult to attack. But why does the warlord Utagawa want Hiro Ono?'

'He wants my father to teach the sumo wrest-lers how to do karate, so that they will be even more powerful. They will kill him if he refuses. So far he's just taught them simple things, but soon he'll have to teach deadly karate secrets. He cannot pretend much longer.'

Hubert had one eye on a strange old woman sitting in one corner of the hall, bent over several pieces of paper. But now he stopped watching to ask how it was that Hiro Junior knew about all this. 'I mean, if Hiro Ono is a prisoner on Tobi-shima, how do you know what is happening to him?'

Lord Oko nodded slowly and looked at Hiro Junior. 'This young man is very wise. He has talked to Nozoki fishermen who know the island well, and they have told him about a cave under the island. At the back of the cave is a tunnel which comes out on the island near Utagawa's castle.'

'I have been there,' said Hiro Junior. 'I know where my father is, but I cannot get him out. That's why he sent for you. It is time to rescue him from the evil Utagawa.'

Belinda turned and grinned at Knackerleevee. 'At last, a real adventure. But where's Hubert?' They looked round the great hall and were just in time to see Hubert disappearing at the far end with the old lady he had watched so closely. Hiro Junior smiled.

'He is with the old lady. I think perhaps it is safer for him.'

Belinda was about to say something in Hubert's defence, but then she realized that Hiro Junior was right. Hubert wasn't a fighter. Her thoughts were interrupted by Lord Oko. He squeezed her arm. 'If you succeed,' he began, 'then you can marry my son, Hi Sing. He will be Lord of Nozoki after me.'

'Thank you very much,' Belinda replied politely. 'But I would rather marry someone I want to marry.' She felt an urgent tug on her sleeve.

'You must not speak like that to Lord Oko. You must agree with everything he says,' Hiro Junior whispered.

'Why?' asked Belinda, getting straight to the point.

But this time she was completely ignored as something far more important was happening – Lord Oko was calling for his servant to bring tea. A lady shuffled silently up to the throne with a tray. There were five delicate cups and a tiny teapot. The smell of jasmine filled the air. Bowing low over the teapot, and never raising her face, the servant poured out the tea. She handed a cup to Belinda.

'There are bits in it!' she whispered loudly.

'Please, you must drink it!' said Hiro Junior. 'They are petals from the jasmine flower.'

'But I always have three lumps of sugar, AND milk!'

'This is Japan. Drink,' said Hiro Junior.

'If I die of poisoning . . .' began Belinda, and she took a sip. It was a very strange brew. On her first sip she thought it was most peculiar. The second she thought was strange, and the third rather nice. 'It's like perfume,' she murmured.

Knackerleevee, who had been ignored so far, gave a grunt and stretched out a hairy hand for one of the tiny cups. The poor servant had never seen a Bogle hand before. She gave a delicate scream, dropped the teapot and ran from the room.

Lord Oko sighed. He kicked off his slippers and rubbed his toes. 'I am surrounded by useless people, and my slippers are too small for me,' he complained.

'Perhaps it is your feet that are too big?' suggested Belinda.

Lord Oko smiled. 'I like you,' he said. 'You will make a fine wife for my son Hi Sing.'

'Thank you all the same, but I've already told you that I shall choose who I marry,' answered Belinda.

Lord Oko rose from his seat and stared into her face. 'So, you come all this way, across seas and oceans. You come all this way to tell me my son Hi Sing is no good?'

Belinda could recognize all the signs of a temper tantrum about to start. She was used to them with her own father. 'No, I didn't say that. I said that I would choose who I marry, and when.' She was secretly wondering why it was that fathers seemed to be set on getting their children married off.

Lord Oko drew in his breath sharply and clapped his hands. Another screen was drawn invisibly back. A chair on poles, carried by eight servants, trotted into the hall. The chair needed eight servants to carry it because seated on it was a hugely fat young man, wrapped in gorgeous silk robes. Lord Oko beamed. 'This is my son Hi Sing. Have you ever seen anyone like him? You see, I am growing my own sumo wrestler.'

Hi Sing waved one chubby arm. 'Hallo Daddy!' he called. 'I've just had thirty-seven doughnuts!' Lord Oko nodded proudly.

'Good boy.' He turned to Belinda. 'This is some prize,' he suggested.

'Yes,' agreed Belinda, who had decided that one word answers were the most likely to keep her out of trouble for the time being. Lord Oko clapped his hands once more.

'Take him away before the young princess is overcome with love,' he ordered. Belinda was saved from further embarrassment by Hiro Junior who stepped forward and told Lord Oko that they really must make their plans and get under way. 'Of course. I wish you all the luck in the world. And when you bring back Hiro Ono, we'll have a wedding!'

Lord Oko left the hall, followed by a vast army of servants and warriors. Belinda was wondering where Hubert had got to, now that they were almost ready to go. Hiro Junior went off to find the painter while Knackerleevee and Belinda thought about their plans for attack.

Eventually Hiro Junior came back, dragging Hubert with him. 'He was with the old lady, folding paper.'

'Origami actually,' said Hubert moodily. 'It's called origami.'

'You've been folding paper?' asked Belinda. 'At a time like this?'

'Well it's better than watching fat old men fall over,' he replied. 'Anyhow, Hiro Junior says you've been asked to marry Hi Sing. Have you seen him? He looks as if he's been made out of marshmallows.'

'What's it to you?' snapped Belinda. 'Who are you to tell me who I can marry? I don't suppose you're even coming to the island, you're such a coward.' She slipped one arm through Hiro Junior's and the two went off, smiling and talking. Hubert was left feeling very small, angry and hurt.

Knackerleevee stopped beside the painter and stared after his mistress. 'I haven't seen her like this before,' grunted the Bogle. 'I think she has a soft spot for Hiro Ono's son.'

Hubert was silent. They were the exact thoughts that filled his heart with cold lead.

5

Deep Dark Dungeons

It was very dark when they set sail for Tobi-shima. There was only a thin crescent moon and the stars to light the sky. 'That's good,' said Hiro Junior. 'It will be difficult for the castle soldiers to spot us.'

Silently they watched the sinister shape of Tobi-shima draw closer. Belinda shivered. Hiro Junior slipped off his coat and gently placed it round her shoulders. 'You are cold,' he murmured. For a moment Belinda looked deeply into his eyes and he gazed steadily back into hers.

Hubert watched and his heart knotted itself even tighter. 'I think I'm going to be sick,' he muttered, and went to the back of the boat, where he watched the dark water churning behind them as the sails filled and the boat sped on.

Hubert was confused and upset. Worst of all, he hated himself. He knew what he was feeling. It was jealousy, and he didn't like it. Why did he have to come all the way to Japan to find out? It was all Hiro Junior's fault. Hubert knew that he loved Belinda. He had never told her. What was the point? He was an artist and she was a princess. Besides, Belinda hardly ever took any notice of him at all.

They had been through many adventures together. Hubert knew he wasn't brave, but there had been no one else for Belinda to turn to or speak with – only himself. Now there was Hiro Junior. Hubert clenched his fists and wished he was a karate expert. All that time he had wasted with that stupid old woman doing origami tricks – what use was that at a time like this?

Feeling very sorry for himself Hubert went back and joined the others. The island was very close now, and all that he could see were huge black cliffs towering in front of them. Hiro Junior was giving instructions.

'There, see beyond that rock that looks like a fish tail. You see the darkness? That is the cave we must sail into.'

Hubert was afraid that the boat would be smashed by the huge waves as they burst over the jagged rocks. But Hiro Junior managed to steer the little vessel carefully past them. For several moments the boat was picked up and hurled round like a marble in a pinball machine, then all at once there was complete calm and they drifted forward into an utterly silent, utterly dark cave.

As the boat moved on to the back of the cave, Knackerleevee lit three lanterns. Here there was a naturally flat shelf of rock. The boat bumped against the edge. They tied up and the rescue party jumped ashore. Belinda turned to Hubert. 'Stay here with the boat,' she whispered. 'If we are not back by morning then sail back to Nozoki and tell Lord Oko.'

Hubert folded his arms. 'I was going to come with you,' he said stonily. Belinda searched his face and put a hand on his shoulder.

'We need someone here Hubert. There may be fighting and, well, you know you are no good at it. If you came I would worry about you getting hurt. Hiro Junior is a karate expert and Knackerleevee can look after himself. So can I. But you . . .' Her words trailed away.

Hubert nodded slowly. She was right, but how he wished she wasn't. He wished he could fight. He wished he was brave. He took one of the lanterns from Knackerleevee. 'I'll wait until

morning,' he said, and a moment later the others had vanished into the darkness of the tunnel.

It seemed to go on for ever. It was not too bad for Hiro Junior and Belinda, but the poor Bogle was getting really battered. He was just a bit too big and bulky to pass through the tunnel in any comfort. He banged his head against the ceiling and his knees and elbows kept rubbing against the sides. As they neared the end Hiro put out the lantern to make sure they were not spotted. Then they all suffered. Belinda gritted her teeth and forced herself not to cry out every time she hit her head on the roof, and she stumbled on in Hiro Junior's footsteps. At last they scrambled up a steep path and suddenly they were standing on open ground. A million stars glittered in the dark sky above.

'It's beautiful,' murmured Belinda. 'I wish Hubert was here.'

'No time for wishing,' hissed Hiro Junior. 'Look, there's the castle.'

Turning round Belinda got quite a different view from the wonderful night sky. Not a stone's throw away rose the massive walls of the castle of the warlord Utagawa. They were smooth and stretched high into the sky. Keeping under the cover of bushes they crept forward, watching the tiny figures of the patrolling guards on the ramparts.

They made a last quick dash and huddled down against the castle walls, safe in its own shadow. Hiro Junior moved along a few paces and then flung himself down by a small barred window that was only just above ground level. 'Hey, father, it is your son Hiro Junior.'

And then Belinda heard the voice that she had not heard for so long, and yet it was a voice that she instantly recognized. 'Hiro Junior? Are you back?'

'Yes, father, and I have brought Little Daughter of Earthquake and Knackerleevee.'

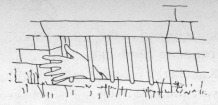

An old, thin hand groped its way between the bars. Belinda grasped it and kissed it warmly. 'I've come Hiro Ono. Are we in time?'

'My heart is full of hope once more,' whispered the old man. 'But you must work quickly. I do not know how you will get me out of this prison.'

'Don't worry father,' said Hiro Junior. 'We have a plan.'

'We have a plan?' repeated Knackerleevee. 'What plan?'

Hiro Junior uncoiled a long rope from his waist. The Bogle shook his head. 'That's not a plan. That's a piece of string.'

Hiro Junior looked at the Bogle in despair. 'I shall climb the wall,' he explained. 'When I reach the top I shall fasten the rope and throw it down to you. Then you can both climb up.'

'But that wall!' Belinda gasped. 'No one could climb that!'

There came the sound of faint laughter from inside the prison and Hiro Ono clutched at the bars. 'You've forgotten my lessons Little Daughter of Earthquake. All things are possible, but some are more possible than others.'

Hiro Junior turned to the wall and began to climb like a spider. Knackerleevee and Belinda were amazed at his speed and agility. In one minute he was halfway to the top. Two more minutes and he was there. He gave a quick wave and disappeared over the parapet. A few moments later a rope came snaking down the wall.

Belinda began to shin up and soon joined Hiro Junior. Then the Bogle grunted and groaned and hauled himself up. The three of them crouched behind a low wall, out of sight of the patrolling guards. Hiro Junior pointed to the doorway of a tower.

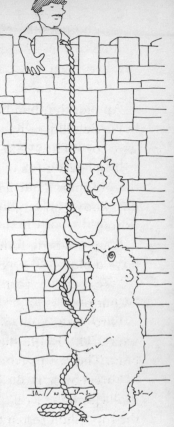

'Those stairs lead straight down to the dungeons,' he whispered. 'First we must deal with these guards.'

The Karate Princess smiled. 'It will be my pleasure,' she murmured, standing up as a guard passed by the wall. 'Haaakk!' There was a dull thud as the guard slipped to the ground. She dragged him behind the wall.

'Who goes there?' grunted a second guard. He came to the wall. Belinda stood up and gave a little curtsey.

'Good evening,' she said politely, and quietly blipped him over the head. He didn't even have time to shout 'help!' or 'mummy!' Meanwhile Hiro Junior and Knackerleevee were seeing to the other guards.

Soon they were all tied up and gagged. The rescuers made for the stairs and tiptoed down. Near the bottom they had to pass the entrance to the main hall. Loud voices came from inside. Belinda peered round the edge of the door.

There was the warlord Utagawa. Belinda's eyes almost popped out with disbelief. The terrible Utagawa was tiny. He was also fat. He had a fat, round squashed up face. Tiny eyes burned from beneath eyebrows like shafts of black lightning. There was no doubt that he was as evil as Hell itself.

One by one the rescuers flattened out against the floor and wriggled across the open doorway. The warlord went on shouting and drinking with his wrestlers and guards. Belinda was the last across. Utagawa's snake-eyes flickered. Then she was safely at the other side. The rescuers went on down the stairs, thankful to leave the noise from the hall behind them.

As they made their way deeper under the castle, there were just a few fading lanterns to light their path. The walls were running with water. Rats scuttled from their feet with sharp squeaks. All at once Hiro Junior stopped and put a finger to his lips. He pointed ahead to a sleeping guard, sitting right outside Hiro Ono's cell. Inside, they could see Hiro Ono standing and waiting silently for them.

Hiro Junior crept forward. There was a sharp blow and the guard slumped to one side, obviously intent on sleeping a lot longer. Belinda whisked the keys from his belt and a few seconds later the cell door was unlocked and she was hugging her old master, Hiro Ono. He had tears in his eyes. 'It has been a long time,' was all he could say.

'Come father,' said Hiro Junior. 'There's no time to talk, we must get going straight away.'

At that moment the cell door was kicked shut. It gave a hollow clang as the locks sprang into place. Standing outside was the warlord Utagawa himself. Knackerleevee roared with rage and launched himself at the thick bars, but it was no use. Utagawa just laughed.

'Such a shame. To come all this way and end up locked in with the old man. Well my friends, there's no hope for you now. I have Hiro Ono. I have his son. I have a Bogle and the famous Karate Princess. No one can stop me now. Did you really think I would not see you doing that silly crawl across my doorway?'

The warlord seized the lantern, snuffed it out and began to walk up the stairs. Suddenly, he stopped and turned around, a wicked grin on his face. 'I shall go to bed now and have lots of nice thoughts about how to kill you all. Good-night. Sweet dreams!'

His footsteps slowly died away and, one by one, he snuffed out the remaining lanterns, until the cell was plunged into a deep black gloom.

6

Man or Mouse?

It was extraordinarily boring sitting in the semi-darkness with nothing to do but twiddle one's thumbs. Hubert had twiddled both thumbs, and all his fingers, for at least five hours. He was beginning to wonder if it was possible to twiddle his big toes, if he took off his socks and shoes.

He walked up and down the stone jetty. Beyond the cave mouth he could see the first signs of dawn. Belinda had told him to wait until dawn and if they were not back by then to sail for Nozoki and get help. But help might not come soon enough.

Hubert was torn between two ideas. Either he could sail for Nozoki, which felt like running away, (except that he was in a boat and you can't run away in a boat), or he could go to the castle and find out what had happened to the rescue party. Hubert began to laugh. He could rescue the rescue party. It was obvious they had been captured or they would have returned by now.

Poor Hubert had one further problem. He was scared. He simply did not like fighting and heroics. If he got a nose-bleed he thought he was going to die. He was not a brave person. All he wanted to do was paint pictures.

A single ray of sunlight flashed above the horizon and shot to the back of the cave. Hubert stared at the brightness and made up his mind. The thought of sailing away from Belinda and leaving her in the lurch was too much. He grabbed the lantern and made his way into the tunnel.

By the time he reached the surface it was getting quite light. Hubert stood and looked at the huge sloping walls of the castle, wondering how to get inside. He had no plan at all. He only knew that he had to rescue the others.

He walked round the castle walls until he found the front gateway. It seemed like as good a way in as any. Finding no doorknocker, Hubert picked up a stone and hammered on the thick wood. The sound echoed through the castle.

Just as Hubert was beginning to think that this might not have been such a good idea there were noises from behind the door. Chains clanged, bolts were drawn and at last the huge doors swung slowly back. Hubert found himself staring at the bulging belly button of a sumo wrestler. He gulped.

'Oh! Um, er, my name is Hubert and I come from over there somewhere and I think you've got my friends here so can I have them back please?' The artist peered up at the wrestler's face. He might just as well have studied a brick. Hubert began to feel small and fragile and stupid. Just as he was beginning to think he had started something very foolish, the wrestler opened his mouth and out came a single word.

'Follow.'

Hubert trotted behind him, looking in every direction with his painter's eye, memorizing the layout of the castle. They went up stairs and down stairs, then up again. At length they came to the main hall. 'Stay!' barked the guard, and

Hubert, feeling rather like a pet dog, stayed. The guard went into the hall. A few moments passed. He came back, picked Hubert from the ground by his collar, carried him into the hall and dropped him at the feet of Utagawa himself.

Hubert sighed. Oh dear, he thought, more problems. Utagawa was seated on a magnificent throne, carved from a single tree trunk in the shape of a pile of twisted bodies. Because he was rather short his feet stuck out over the edge and could not reach the floor. Hubert stared at them.

'What are you looking at?' growled the war-lord. 'You dare to gaze upon the feet of the mighty Utagawa?'

'No, no,' began Hubert.

'Then what do you want, tiny person?'

Hubert thought his last remark was a bit much coming from a dwarf such as Utagawa himself, but since Hubert was surrounded by at least twenty sumo wrestlers he decided to let it pass.

'I've come for my friends,' he said simply, and inwardly kicked himself for being so stupid.

Utagawa laughed. 'You must be unbelievably mad. You knock on my door and ask for your friends back. Do you know what I am going to do to your friends?'

'Well, it's quite early in the morning, so I hope you are going to offer them some breakfast.'

The warlord went cross-eyed with rage. He drew his sword and waved the mighty weapon in Hubert's face.

Hubert was surprised at how brave he was beginning to feel, faced with this short-tempered monster. He grabbed the tip of the blade with one finger and thumb and drew it down his cheek. 'I could do with a shave,' he murmured.

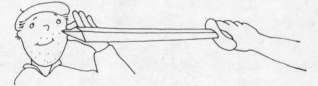

Utagawa slowly turned purple. His eyes narrowed and his face became a dangerous scowl. (Actually, Hubert thought it looked more like a tomato slowly growing mouldy.) He clapped his hands and the room was suddenly swarming with guards. Utagawa turned to them. 'Take this poor fool away and put him with the others. And make sure they are all extremely uncomfortable!'

Hubert stopped smiling. It was now or never. As the sumo wrestlers closed in round him he took a deep breath, closed his eyes, pinched his nose and summoned up all he had been taught about the Inner Origami. In the still silence of his mind, he quietly folded himself into a chair.

Uproar followed as the stunned guards searched the room. The warlord was on his feet in an apoplexy of rage. 'Fools! You've let him escape. Find him at once!' The guards stumbled round, looking under the throne, bumping into each other and scratching their heads. One knocked over a chair that hadn't been there earlier. The chair crawled straight for the door.

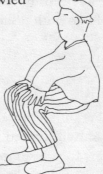

Utagawa screamed. 'There he goes! After him!' Hubert was on his feet in a flash. He had an advantage over the guards. They were so huge it slowed them down and they got in each other's way. Hubert raced down the passage, with the sumo wrestlers thundering behind like hungry dinosaurs. Hubert knew that the others must be down in the dungeons somewhere. He almost fell down the spiral stairs, taking them three at a time, four at a time, and then six, before crashing into the door at the bottom.

He jumped to his feet quickly and looked around – he was in the kitchen. The castle cooks turned in surprise and began to wave pans at him. The stairs behind rang with the stampeding wrestlers. Hubert plucked up courage and raced for safety, screaming. 'Aaaaaaaaaaaaaaaaarrrgh!'

The cooks fell this way and that as Hubert charged through. Pans went up in the air, somer-saulting and emptying their contents on to the pursuing guards. A great downpour of noodles rained upon them. Hubert raced out through the

door at the far end while the guards
struggled to free themselves from the sticky
noodle ribbons.

Hubert was now some distance ahead.
He leaned against a wall, panting violently
and trying to get his head clear. There
were more spiral stairs ahead. Hubert crossed
his fingers and took them eight at a time.

Behind him came the wrestlers, with streams of
noodles flapping from every limb. Behind them
came an army of cooks, waving saucepans and
knives and noodle forks.

Behind them came the guards. They didn't
know what all the fuss was about but had joined
in anyway.

'What are we chasing?' asked one.

'No idea. Would you like one
of my liquorice allsorts?'

'Thank you very much.' They stumbled on down the stairs.

Way up in front, Hubert was going so fast he had lost control of his legs. He bounced off the curved walls, tripped, fell, rolled, banged and finally went flying straight into the lap of the dungeon guard, knocking him out as he did so.

Everyone in the cell jumped to their feet. 'Hubert! Brilliant! Quick – the keys!' Half dazed himself, Hubert grabbed the keys and opened the cell door. But before he could fling it open the first sumo wrestler arrived.

Hubert breathed deeply, held his nose, and silently became a chair once more. The wrestler blinked and shook his head. He wandered across to the cell door. The Karate Princess seized her chance and pushed it open with such force that the wrestler went stumbling backwards, hit his head on the wall and slumped to the floor. Belinda, Hiro Junior and Hiro Ono and the Bogle were out in an instant. They flattened against the wall as the other wrestlers, cooks and guards filled the dungeons.

'Where are they? They've escaped! Search the cells!' Bits of noodle flapped wildly from their arms.

The chair suddenly came back to life and slammed the cell door shut, locking them all inside. Hubert turned to the others with a big grin. They were still staring at the spot where a moment earlier a rather elegant chair had been.

'Was that . . .?' began Belinda. She shook her head.

Only Hiro Ono understood. He looked at Hubert and nodded his old, grey head. 'One day,' he said, 'you will be master.'

'Master of what?' asked Belinda.

'We haven't time,' shouted Hubert. 'Come on, let's go.'

They sped up the stairs and out across the courtyard. Behind them, from the depths of the castle came a growing roar as the sumo wrestlers of Tobi-shima tried to escape. And from the other side of the courtyard came another little army of guards. The ground shook beneath their feet. 'Make for the gate!' yelled Hubert. 'Get it open!'

The Bogle had a better idea. His legs pounded the earth and he headed for the mighty gate at

top speed. 'HAAAAAA-UNKK!' He crunched straight through the thick wood, leaving a gaping, splintered hole for the others to tumble through.

The sumo wrestlers were not far behind and now there seemed to be hundreds of them. Arrows and spears, stones, saucepans, clods of turf, noodle forks, old potatoes, beetles, bits of worm – all came hurtling after the escapees as they raced for the tunnel. They spilled into the little fishing boat, seized the oars and pulled away from the jetty.

As they reached the mouth of the cave and the open sea a hundred furious sumo wrestlers poured on to the jetty, knocking the front four rows straight into the frothing water. Behind them was the warlord Utagawa himself. He pushed his way between their legs and stood there screaming and waving his sword. 'You won't escape!' he yelled. 'I shall crush you to nothing!'

7

The Biggest Question of All

The five friends were triumphant. As the fishing boat headed back to Nozoki they held hands and danced round and round. 'But how did you do it Hubert?' Belinda asked breathlessly. 'I mean one minute you were there and then you weren't – there was just something strange. You vanished.'

Hubert grinned like a monkey. Even Hiro Ono smiled encouragement at the young artist. 'There's more to the painter than meets the eye,' said the old man. 'I think maybe Hubert met the old woman, Konomatai?'

'She's amazing,' agreed Hubert. 'She's incredibly old and . . .'

'The incredibly old woman, Konomatai, you speak of is my wife,' said Hiro Ono.

Hubert reddened. Then he went redder. Finally he was so embarrassed that Hiro Ono had to start laughing. 'It doesn't matter – Hiro Ono is an incredibly old man!'

Hubert muttered an apology and went on. 'I saw this woman doing some paper folding – origami – and went to see. She dragged me off somewhere – that was where I went all that time at the palace. She taught me the secret origami. You know origami is the art of folding paper, but for centuries there has been this secret art, called Inner Origami, where you fold yourself.'

Belinda frowned. 'What on earth do you mean Hubert?' Hiro Ono smiled and took her hand.

'It is simple Little Daughter. Your young friend means that he can fold himself – like – so!' Before their eyes Hiro Ono seemed to disappear. All they could see was a small table that had not been there before. Then the table slowly unfolded and Hiro Ono reappeared. Belinda sat down heavily.

'That's incredible!' she whispered.

'It's a question of believing in yourself, like karate,' said Hiro Ono. 'It is also a question of disbelief. Nobody believes that a person can change into a table so when it happens they don't see it.'

Knackerleevee tapped Hiro Ono on his bony shoulder. 'Could you explain all that again. I still don't understand.'

'Hubert, can you really do this?' asked Belinda. The young artist pinched his nose, turned himself into a chair, unfolded and reappeared. 'That's fantastic!' Belinda had turned quite pale. Hiro Ono watched her with amusement.

'I can only do chairs so far,' Hubert said humbly. 'Konomatai was going to teach me more but we had to leave then.'

Belinda threw her arms round Hubert and kissed him. 'Hubert, you saved us. I don't believe it. Thank you.' Hubert grinned, looked even more like a delighted monkey and got so red he had to go and stand at the back of the ship and stare out to sea for ten minutes. It was just as well he did for he spotted at least fifty warships fast catching them in the stiff wind.

'Put up more sail!' yelled Hiro Junior. A black blur fell from the sky and perched on the rail.

'Never fear,' cried Crow. 'It is I, the karate wonderbird. With one blow of my wing I shall send the . . .'

'OH SHUT UP WILL YOU!' cried everyone at once. Crow's beak snapped shut. Then opened again. But before she could say more there was a hollow boom in the distance and a puff of smoke. A cannonball whizzed overhead and plunged into the sea. A few seconds later several more came, buzzing past like giant bees. The boat rocked violently from the splashes but wasn't hit.

As the vessel touched the wooden pier everyone jumped out and raced up the path to the palace. Some distance behind two hundred sumo wrestlers leapt into the water and came plunging up the beach after them. Brave Crow took one look at the mountains of heaving flesh and decided she would see how fast she could fly in the opposite direction.

Utagawa was sitting high on the shoulders of one of his wrestlers, waving his huge sword and yelling at his men. 'After them, kill them! Cut them into little bits! Make jam out of them! Fry them with noodles!' He poked his mount with his sword. 'Go faster you fool!' The wrestler stumbled on through the waves, lost his balance and threw the warlord into the foaming sea.

Belinda, Hubert, Knackerleevee, Hiro Ono and Hiro Junior ran panting into the palace. Lord Oko had already seen what was happening. His karate warriors were lined up ready to fight. Even the two old sumo wrestlers had come out, although one was in a wheelchair. They lined the walls, ready to repel any attackers. Knackerleevee grunted and turned to Belinda.

'This will be some battle eh, Princessnesty?'

'Take care old friend,' Belinda replied. She glanced across at Hiro Junior. He was speaking calmly to each of his karate warriors. Once again Belinda found herself thinking how strong and handsome he was.

The gates thundered and shook as the sumo

wrestlers of Tobi-shima came up against them and began to batter the foundations. The pillars creaked and groaned. They could not take the pressure for ever. The thunder grew to a crescendo and with a squeal of splintered wood the doors fell down flat. A cloud of dust rose from the ground and through it poured two hundred sumo wrestlers, stamping and snorting like bulls.

Hubert had no time to feel fear. Faced with a sumo wrestler heading straight for him, he did the only thing he could and folded into a chair. The wrestler stopped and scratched his head. He looked behind to see if Hubert was there and at that moment the chair sprang into action. Hubert leapt from the ground and clambered up the wrestler's back. He sat astride his shoulders and wrapped his arms tightly round the wrestler's eyes.

The wrestler heaved and jumped and ran wild, cannoning into other wrestlers and knocking them flying. 'Yeee-ha!' yelled Hubert, filled with excitement and fear at the same time.

Around him a tremendous battle was taking place. The karate warriors launched themselves at the waves of wrestlers. The air was thick with cries of 'Haaa-akk!' But it was no use. The karate warriors were slowly being driven back towards the palace. Hubert saw Hiro Junior disappear beneath the legs of a wrestler. He was caught and flung up the path where he landed with the breath knocked from his body. He staggered back into the battle.

Knackerleevee was the only one having any real success. He was using his sheer size and strength to take on the sumos at their own game. Already there was a pile of unconscious bodies round him, but now he was being attacked from

all sides. Hubert saw the brave Bogle stagger from a welter of blows.

There was a cry from Belinda as she was caught by a giant sumo wrestler and crushed in his arms. Without stopping to think Hubert let go of his mount and slid to the ground. He raced over and tried to pull the locked arms away from the princess. The wrestler raised one thick leg and kicked Hubert away as if he were an annoying little fly.

Hubert sprawled in the dust. Desperate to save Belinda he came straight back at the wrestler grabbing at anything to stop him. He tugged on the tasselled strings of the sumo's trunks. There was a strange 'schloopeedoop' sound. Hubert suddenly found himself holding a handful of very long laces. The sumo wrestler gave a gargled cry as his trunks almost fell down. He dropped the Karate Princess to the ground and hurried off clutching his trunks in both hands.

Hubert stared at the laces and then at the rapidly retreating wrestler. He grabbed Belinda and pulled her to her feet. 'Pull the laces!' he cried. 'Pull the laces!' Another wrestler was almost upon them. With a lightning flash of one hand Hubert tugged away another handful of tassels.

'Eeek!' squeaked the wrestler, grabbing his falling trunks. He ran off, straight after the first one. Belinda grinned with delight and the two of them waded back into battle. Now a new cry could be heard.

'Pull the laces!' Even Crow joined in, flying over the clouds of dust, the thuds and the groans. 'Pull the laces!' she squawked, again and again. Then there came the squeals of shame.

'Ooooh!'

'Aaah! 'Scuse me a minute!' The wrestlers began to flee. Some were luckier than others and managed to catch their trunks just in time. Belinda pretended that she hadn't seen the others.

The karate warriors of Nozoki soon got the idea and before long the entire sumo army was running away from Belinda and Hubert and their band. Only the warlord Utagawa stood his ground, until at last he was mown down by fifteen of his own men. All Knackerleevee had to do was pick up the warlord semi-conscious from the ground. Hiro Junior dusted him down.

'It's the dungeon for you, Utagawa.'

'My wrestlers are all disgraced,' hissed the

warlord as he was handed over to a group of karate warriors and led away. It was all over. The companions looked round at the battleground and grinned at each other. Belinda looked thoughtfully at young Hiro Junior. He flashed back a smile. She looked at Hubert. She wanted to say something but didn't know how to start or what words to use. It was Hiro Ono who filled the dusty silence.

'Many things happen in battle,' he said. 'Sometimes we find peace in the middle of war. Sometimes we find out something about ourselves that we didn't know before. Sometimes we discover something about other people too. Come Hiro Junior my son, we must go and see if your mother is safe.'

Belinda watched the old man go, with his strong son holding him round the waist. 'He's extraordinary. He knows what you are thinking before you even think it. How did he know?'

'How did he know what Princessness?' growled Knackerleevee.

The Karate Princess swallowed hard and tried to find the courage – more courage than she had ever needed before. She felt as if she was stepping off a cliff blindfolded. She turned to Hubert. Her words came out like a croak.

'Would you marry me, Hubert? Please?'

For a second there was a breathless hush. Then

there came a small thud, quickly followed by a much louder one. First Hubert, then Knacker-leevee, fainted.

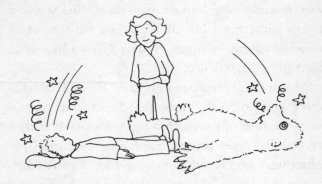